Written and Illustrated by BILL PEET

Hubert's Hair-Raising Adventure

HOUGHTON MIFFLIN COMPANY BOSTON

Library of Congress catalog card number: 59-7478
ISBN: 0-395-15083-3
ISBN: 0-395-28267-5 (pbk.)

Printed in the United States of America

WOZ   30   29   28   27   26   25   24   23

Hubert the Lion was haughty and vain
And especially proud of his elegant mane.

But conceit of this sort isn't proper at all
And Hubert the Lion was due for a fall.
One day as he sharpened his claws on a rock
He received a most horrible, terrible shock.
A flaming hot spark flew up into the air,
Came down on his head and ignited his hair.

With a roar of surprise he took off like a streak,
Away through the jungle to Zamboozi Creek.
He leaped in kersplash! with a shower of bubbles,
And came bobbing up with a head full of stubbles.

At first he just stared with a wide-open mouth
At the cloud of black smoke drifting off to the south.
Then he felt with his paws just in back of his ears
And he suddenly realized the worst of his fears.

"I'm ruined," he shouted, "oh what'll I do!
I'd rather be dead or go live in a zoo!
And if anyone sees me, oh what a disgrace,
So I'd better discover a good hiding place!"

He looked all around till he finally spied
An old hollow tree with a hole in one side.
He squeezed himself in but the fit was too tight,
The last half of Hubert was still in plain sight.

Along came a Bird with a very large beak
And asked if she too could play hide-and-go-seek.
It was nosy old Hornbill who everyone knew
Was the neighborhood gossip with nothing to do.
Her eggs were all hatched and her children had grown,
So now she made everyone's business her own.

"Good gracious," she said when she peeked in the tree.
"Your mane's disappeared! You're bald as can be.
How did it happen? I've just got to know.
Please tell me, Hubert, and then I must go."
So the Lion related with obvious pain
How he'd managed to burn off his elegant mane.
"I must say," said the Bird, "that it's really absurd!
But I'll keep it a secret. I won't say a word."
Then she fluttered away just as fast as she could
To broadcast the news to the whole neighborhood.

And so in just about no time at all
A group of his friends came to pay him a call.
A wrinkled old Elephant and a Giraffe,
A Hyena with spots and a snickering laugh,
A Zebra, a Rhino, a skinny old Gnu,
A Leopard, and finally the Hornbill Bird too.

"Come out," called the Bird, "and let everyone see."
But there wasn't a sound from the old hollow tree.
"Please," said the Elephant, "we won't make fun.
We're here to consider just what can be done."
"You've no need to be shy," said the gawky Giraffe.
"The Hyena's promised he'll try not to laugh."

So Hubert crawled outside to show them his trouble
And sighed, "You can see that there's nothing but stubble."
"A most serious problem," the Elephant said
As he studied the surface of poor Hubert's head.
"It will never grow back, you can be pretty sure,
Unless we can manage to think of some cure."

"We could make," said the Zebra, "a wig out of weeds."
"Or find," said the Rhino, "some hair-growing seeds."
"With some cloth," said the Gnu, "and a needle and thread
We could sew a big cap that would cover his head."
"I know!" said the Elephant. "Wait just a minute!
 I remember a cure but I can't think what's in it."
He thought and he thought and he flapped his big ears.
Then he finally said, "It is crocodile tears!"

"There's a Croc in the swamp," said the Bird with the Bill.
"And he lives just a mile west of Old Monkey Hill."
"It's a horrible place," said the Gnu with a groan.
"And a spot," said the Leopard, "that's best left alone."
"Come *on!*" said the Elephant, "don't be faint-hearted.
Just hand me that bucket. It's time we got started."

"I think that I'd better not go," said the Gnu.
"You know I'm just over a case of the flu."
And the Leopard said, "I've a sore spot on my toe.
If it wasn't for that I would just love to go."
"I have a stiff neck," said the gawky Giraffe.
"Me too," the Hyena put in with a laugh.
"I'm afraid," said the Rhino, "I'd be in the way."
"I'll go," said the Zebra, "but some other day."
So the Elephant said with a look of disgust,
"I suppose I can go by myself if I must."
And he lumbered away down the dark forest trail,
Flapping his ears and switching his tail.

The going was easy the first mile or two,
Except for some trees he could barely squeeze through.
Then he made a sharp turn and the trail disappeared.
He had come to the swamp, to the place they all feared.
And he stopped for a second, one moment of dread,
Then he thought of poor Hubert and forged on ahead.
He plowed like a tank through the tangles of brush
And he struggled through mud that was thick as cold mush.
Till he saw a deep pool through the mist and the fog
And in the dark water an old rotten log.

But logs have no eyes, and as everyone knows,
No ugly fat flippers, or scaly green toes,
Or long rows of teeth that stick out when they smile,
But *this* log of course was a big Crocodile.
"Good day," said the crafty and creepy old Croc
As he slowly crept out to recline on a rock.
"And what brings you here, Mr. Flapperjack Ears?"
The Elephant said, "Just to borrow some tears."
"I'm sorry," the crafty Croc said with a sigh,
"But I never shed tears and it's useless to try.
Why, only last week as I swam in the lake
I swallowed a very dear friend by mistake.
At the time I admit that I felt some regret,
For you see my poor stomach was slightly upset.
But I have an old saying that's ever so true:
'You can't have your friends and eat them all too.'

But what do you want now with crocodile tears?
You really don't think that they'll shrink your big ears?"
"Oh no," said the Elephant, "they aren't for me.
The tears are for Hubert the Lion, you see."
Then he told about Hubert, not changing a word
Of the story he'd heard from the nosy old Bird.

Now as the Croc listened he started to grin
From in back of his eyes all the way to his chin.
And then all at once he threw open his jaws
And exploded with laughter in great loud guffaws.
He held both his sides and he staggered around
Until soon he was flopping all over the ground.
And the Elephant saw, to his happy surprise,
That tears started to come to the Crocodile's eyes.

They rolled down his long face all sparkling and green
Like beautiful emeralds fit for a queen
And they dropped in the bucket just under his chin
That the Elephant put there to capture them in.
And when the old Croc at last managed to stop,
The bucket was filled pretty near to the top.

"That's fine," said the Elephant, "now if I'm right
Poor Hubert will have his new mane by tonight.
So thank you, my friend, you are very kind-hearted."
And then with a hasty "goodbye" he departed.

The long journey back was a difficult trick
With a bucket to carry and fog growing thick.
And with great swarms of gnats flying into his face
He crept through the swamp at a very slow pace.
He tripped on a Hippo and bruised his left knee
And tattered one ear on a prickle-thorn tree
But strangely enough he completed the trip
Without tipping the bucket or spilling one drip.

His friends were amazed and they had to confess
That they'd never expected one ounce of success.
"Please tell us," they said, "how on earth did you do it?"
"An old trick," said the Elephant, "nothing much to it."
"Come, Hubert," he said, "soak your paws in the tears
And rub on your head everywhere but your ears.
And now then," he added when this was completed,
"You'd better relax and get comfortably seated."

So Hubert climbed onto a boulder nearby,
Where he sat very still staring up at the sky,
While his friends sat around him all ready to shout
At the very first sign of his new mane to sprout.

One minute passed by and then two and three
But still Hubert's head was as bare as could be.
"It's no use," said the Bird, "it's a foolish mistake."
"That's right," said the Rhino, "it's all a big fake."
"Or a horrible joke," said the gawky Giraffe.
So the Hyena laughed his most horrible laugh,
But the Elephant said, "It's still too soon to tell.
This hair-growing business might take quite a spell."
"You mean," said the Zebra, "a whole hour or two."
"Or maybe ten years," said the skinny old Gnu.

They watched and they waited till way after nine
But still nothing happened. Not even a sign.
At last they grew sleepy and then pretty soon
There was no one to watch but a big yellow moon.
And with no one to question, and no one to doubt,
Hubert's bare head was beginning to sprout!
It grew very thick and it grew very fast
And before even more than ten seconds had passed,
The elegant mane was completely restored
While its owner poor Hubert slept soundly and snored.

But I'm sorry to say that it didn't stop there,
It was only the start of this fast-growing hair.
It spiraled straight up in a great golden crest
Then off to the south, to the north, east and west.
It went swirling and curling and crawling and creeping
All over his friends who were still soundly sleeping.
It curled round their feet and it swirled round their knees,
It crawled up their backs and then up through the trees.
Then it spread through the jungle in great golden waves
Around bushes and boulders and on into caves.
When the tears were used up then the growing diminished
And Hubert's remarkable mane became finished.

Next day, in a tree where she'd perched for the night,
The Hornbill awoke to this very strange sight.
"Oh dear me!" she cried, with a wail of despair.
"The whole world is totally covered with hair!
Oh please wake up, Hubert! Wake up, everyone!
And see what your crocodile-tear cure has done!"
They all wakened slowly with yawns and deep sighs,
All groaning and stretching and rubbing their eyes.
Then they stared for a second with mouths open wide.
"Jumping Jehosaphat!" somebody cried.
"It's fantastic," said Hubert, "amazing indeed!
But you know there's a little bit more than I need!"
"It's a mess," moaned the Rhino. "A horrible bungle."
"Just look," groaned the Gnu, "it's all over the jungle!"
"We're trapped," cried the Zebra, "oh what can we do?
We've got to get out of this tangled-up stew."

Then they all got excited and started to riot.
Except for the Elephant. He shouted, "Quiet!
Please stop it," he pleaded, "we're getting nowhere!"
"Besides," cried poor Hubert, "you're pulling my hair!"
In a crazy mad scramble they thrashed and they plunged.
They kicked and they butted. They leaped and they lunged.
But the more they all struggled the more they got wrapped
In the big knots and tangles that had them all trapped.

"We're stuck," said the Elephant, "now what we need
Is some scissors if ever we're going to be freed."
"The Baboon," said the Bird, "has a rusty old pair.
And not only that but he loves to cut hair.
And if you'll all promise you'll not go away
I'll fetch him right now without further delay."

But she couldn't fly straight off to Old Monkey Hill,
Not with a beak full of gossip to spill,
And I'm sorry to say it was late afternoon
Before she returned with the Barber Baboon.
For a while the old Monkey sat rubbing his chin,
It was hard to decide where he ought to begin.
At last with a flourish he started in clipping,
His rusty old scissors a-squeaking and snipping.
He lopped off whole armfuls of wavy gold locks
And stacked all the trimmings in big golden shocks.
He lined them in rows very tidy and neat,
Much the same way as the farmers stack wheat.
But as he progressed it required more care
To avoid ears and tails that were mixed in the hair.
Sometimes he slipped with the rusty old shears
And he snipped a few nicks in the Elephant's ears,
And he clipped off the tip of the tail of the Gnu
And the Leopard lost whiskers, in fact all but two.

Then finally he came to the last pile of hair.

"Watch out," said the Elephant, "Hubert's in there."

The Barber clipped on till the job was all done.

"There now," he said, "does it please everyone?"

"It's too round," said the Bird, "take some more off the top.

Then a bit off the sides, then I think you can stop."

So he clipped a big scissorful straight off the crown

And then from the ears he went snipping straight down.

The Elephant said, "That's no way to cut hair!
For now I'm afraid it's entirely too square!"
"Oh please stop," said Hubert, "I'm sure it will do.
There'll be nothing left by the time you're all through.

And besides," he went on with a very smug smile,
"I always have wanted my own special style.
I'm prouder than ever and think you'll agree
That there's no other lion exactly like me.
You can search every jungle, each circus and zoo,
From San Francisco to Timbuctoo
But I doubt that you'll find though you look everywhere
A lion whose mane is so perfectly square.
.... So there!"